MW00995788

Twelve Dancing Unicorns

For my grandmother, who always believed—A.H.

For Annie—J.G.

STERLING CHILDREN'S BOOKS
New York

An Imprint of Sterling Publishing
387 Park Avenue South
New York, NY 10016

ISBN 978-1-4027-8732-4

Library of Congress Cataloging-in-Publication Data

Heyman, Alissa.
Twelve dancing unicorns / Alissa Heyman ; illustrated by Justin Gerard.
p. cm.
Summary: The king's beloved unicorns are hiding a secret and a little girl is determined to solve the mystery.
ISBN 978-1-4027-8732-4 (hardcover)
[1. Fairy tales. 2. Unicorns--Fiction.] I. Gerard, Justin, ill. II. Title.
PZ8.H49Tw 2013
[E]--dc23

2012016408

Distributed in Canada by Sterling Publishing
c/o Canadian Manda Group, 165 Dufferin Street
Toronto, Ontario, Canada M6K 3H6
Distributed in the United Kingdom by GMC Distribution Services
Castle Place, 166 High Street, Lewes, East Sussex, England BN7 1XU
Distributed in Australia by Capricorn Link (Australia) Pty. Ltd.
P.O. Box 704, Windsor, NSW 2756, Australia

Designed by Jennifer Browning and Andrea Miller

For information about custom editions, special sales, and premium and corporate purchases, please contact Sterling Special Sales at 800-805-5489 or specialsales@sterlingpublishing.com.

Printed in China
Lot #:
4 6 8 10 9 7 5 3
04/17

www.sterlingpublishing.com/kids

Twelve Dancing Unicorns

By Alissa Heyman

Illustrated by Justin Gerard

STERLING CHILDREN'S BOOKS
New York

ong ago, there lived a king who was renowned for his magnificent royal gardens. They were filled with dazzling flowers, gilded walkways, and rare animals. Monkeys chattered, tigers growled, and peacocks spread their iridescent tails. But the king's most wondrous creatures were the twelve white unicorns that stood proudly behind a fence, each one attached to its own pomegranate tree by a shining golden chain.

The unicorns were wild, untamable creatures, and they would pace restlessly in their corral. The king treasured his unicorns, and he felt a kinship with their majestic, spirited natures.

One thing troubled the king deeply: Every morning he would find his precious unicorns sleeping peacefully—with their golden chains shattered on the ground. Every day the king's goldsmiths forged new chains to replace the broken ones. Every night the king posted his guards in the unicorns' corral to watch the creatures, but each morning the guards would report that they had seen nothing unusual. They could never explain how the unicorns' chains had been broken.

Villagers came from miles around to see the splendor of the king's unicorns. The crowds were amazed by the magical creatures who shimmered as they moved.

One young girl who visited every day fell especially in love with the smallest unicorn, the most radiant one of all. Sometimes the little unicorn pranced over to the fence, straining at its chain. The girl was able to gently pat its velvety head through the fence and look into its sad sapphire eyes.

As the weeks passed, the king became so desperate to learn the truth of his unicorns' secret that he made a royal declaration: "Whoever from my kingdom can solve the mystery of my unicorns' broken chains in three days' time will be rewarded with a gift of their choosing."

At once, the little girl knew she had to learn the magnificent unicorns' most treasured secret. She saw that the creatures were unhappy being penned up and hoped solving the mystery might allow her to help them.

"My lord, I can discover the unicorns' secret," the little girl told the king, stepping out from the crowd.

Some of the villagers laughed, but the king looked at her and said, "You make a bold claim, but how can you, a mere girl, discover what my brave guards cannot? This is a challenge for someone far beyond your years."

The girl's mother took her by the hand and led her away. But despite the king's words, the girl was determined to find out what the unicorns were hiding.

At home that night, the little girl's mother gave her a magic cloak made from gossamer. It was as sheer and delicate as butterfly wings.

"This cloak was given to me a long time ago by an old woman who I helped in the forest," the girl's mother explained. "She told me to save it for an important occasion, so I want you to have it now. Wear it to the royal castle and you will be invisible."

The girl kissed her mother, put on the cloak, and ran back to the royal gardens as the moon rose high above the castle walls. The girl quietly slipped between the slats of the fence.

Just as they did every night, the king's guards stood at their post inside the unicorns' corral. The unicorns paced as far as their golden chains would let them, their long, white necks straining against their bindings. The girl crouched down and watched.

At the first stroke of midnight, the unicorns turned to the guards and stood very still. They lowered their heads and gave one shake of their enchanted silver horns. The guards froze as if they had turned to stone. Then when the clock tower struck twelve, the golden chains that bound the magnificent creatures shattered like splintering ice.

Under a crescent moon, the unicorns began to dig a large hole in the middle of the corral with their powerful hooves. Then, one by one, each unicorn pranced into the tunnel and disappeared. The smallest unicorn was the last to go. It turned and looked in the girl's direction before disappearing down the hole.

The little girl couldn't believe her eyes!

Hidden by the magic cloak, the girl followed the unicorns down the tunnel.

At the bottom, there was a beautiful glade surrounded by trees. Twinkling from the tree branches were plums made of amethyst. Nearby, a waterfall flowed into a silvery pool and golden flowers sparkled in the grass.

The girl plucked a plum as a token for the king—proof of this enchanted world—and put it in her cloak pocket.

To her amazement, eleven fairies in beautiful gowns flew out of the woods. They fed the unicorns amethyst plums, brought water from the waterfall for them to drink, and braided flowers into their manes.

Then the fairies fluttered onto the backs of all but the smallest unicorn. The creatures began swaying and swirling in the moonlight, faster and faster, prancing and leaping, dashing and twirling. The little girl gasped in surprise. The unicorns were dancing!

As they moved, a symphony of horns and trumpets and tinkling bells filled the enchanted forest. The magical animals whirled by the invisible girl, all except the littlest unicorn who paused and knelt before her.

Without hesitation, the girl jumped onto its back and lost herself in the wild joy of the unicorns' dance.

When the first rose-light of dawn crept across the sky, the twelve unicorns left the enchanted glade and trotted under the amethyst plum trees, through the tunnel, and back up into the king's corral. The little girl followed silently behind, and then the unicorns pawed the loose earth back into place, completely covering the hole.

All but the smallest unicorn settled down to rest. Instead, it turned to the girl and shook its silver mane. She nodded back, and then it too settled down. The girl slipped past the guards who were still under the unicorns' spell.

The next night, the girl put on her magic cloak and returned to the royal gardens. This time when she followed the unicorns into the glade, the trees were heavy with giant ruby cherries. She put some in her pocket.

Then the girl fed and brushed the smallest unicorn herself. When it was time to dance, she again climbed onto its back. The dancing was even faster than the night before, the dashing and whirling even wilder.

On the third night, the trees were bursting with golden apples, and the girl slid one into her pocket. She fed some fruit to the smallest unicorn, combed its flowing mane, and made flower garlands for its head. And then the little girl danced with the beautiful creatures, leaping through the multicolored sky atop her unicorn.

On her way back to the castle, the girl's magic cloak must have slipped a little from her shoulders. To her surprise, a fairy approached her and whispered in her ear, "This glade is the source of the unicorns' powers. Without the jeweled fruit and cascading water, their magic will weaken and fade. The unicorns will wither away unless they are set free. Any human who helps them is allowed to enter this world, which is why you can be here."

When she returned to the king's corral on that third night, the little girl was so weary and sad that she lay down on the ground and fell asleep. The smallest unicorn lay beside her, its head in her lap.

And that's how the king found them when he checked on his unicorns in the morning.

Awakened by the king's arrival, the girl threw off her cloak. "I know the secret of the unicorns, my lord." She told the king the whole story and showed him the jeweled fruit.

"These are remarkable! This fruit is as rare as my magnificent unicorns and must have come from a magical place." The king turned to the girl. "Well, young lady, you have discovered the secret. What would you like as your reward?"

"I would like you to set all twelve unicorns free," she announced.

"I cannot possibly do that!" the king said, looking at his prized creatures. "Having them is my greatest pleasure."

"But without the enchanted forest, the unicorns will weaken and die," the little girl explained. "If you help them now, you may visit them there."

The king lowered his eyes. Then he looked again at his magnificent unicorns. He knew what he had to do. The king ordered his guards to remove the unicorns' golden chains. The magical creatures tossed their proud white manes, dug a deep hole in the ground, and disappeared—all except the smallest unicorn, who trotted over to the little girl.

"Perhaps this unicorn is strong enough to live in our world as long as it returns underground every night," said the king. "Love is a powerful magic.

"Would you like to stay with your special friend?" the king added.

"More than anything," said the girl.

And so it was decided that the smallest unicorn would live with the girl. Wherever they went, the little girl rode on the back of the prancing unicorn, with the delightful sounds of horns and trumpets and tinkling bells filling her ears.

And every night in the enchanted glade, the girl, the king, and the fairies whirled and twirled in the moonlight with the twelve dancing unicorns.